Blank and Other Stories

Femdom Mind Control

Flash Fiction – Vol. 40

S.B.

Disclaimer

This is a work of fiction. Names, characters, business, events, and incidents are the products of the author's imagination. Any resemblance to actual persons, living or dead, or actual events is purely coincidental. All characters are over 18.

Table of Contents

Afraid of Scissors

For as long as he could remember, Xavier had been afraid of scissors. If asked why he couldn't explain it and he preferred not to dwell on the subject, which was often easier said than done. The phobia caused him a lot of grievances growing up, but the major problems arose whenever he needed a haircut. It was either a pair of clippers and a shaver or nothing, preferably in the sanctity of his own home, and the results, while not terrible, were not that great either. His friends often mocked him for his sense of style, but Kyle was an honorable exception.

"The top of your head has seen better days, my friend," he declared one day over a peanut butter sandwich. "We need to get you sorted, a.s.a.p., and I know just the thing you need?"

"Please, not another barbette!" Xavier responded. "I don't have the patience for your insane choices anymore."

"There's nothing insane about Julie, trust me. Once she starts working with you, you'll want no one else, I promise."

"That's what you always say about any cute girl that catches your eye."

"Wrong. That's what I used to say, but now I've seen the truth. She's the best and I would like to prove it. Let me set up an appointment for you and if you're not happy with her work, I'll..."

"You'll what?"

"I'll pay for your breakfast every day until the end of the year. Deal?"

"That's a lot of money, dude. Are you sure you want to do this?"

"Absolutely. Now, give me a shake to seal the deal."

Said and done. Kyle made the reservation in his name for the following Saturday and was all giddy after hanging up the phone as if he were a timid schoolboy experiencing his first crush. Xavier simply nodded, knowing deep in his heart his friend would regret his actions sooner than later. However, sometimes the heart is wrong.

Julie's barbershop stood five blocks away from his home and was the cutest little corner he had ever seen. The sole proprietor of the establishment, she was a slender brunette of South Asian descent with the reputation of having the sultriest smile that ever graced that side of the Pacific and, for once, the rumors weren't misplaced. Despite being dressed in black from head to toe, she irradiated light and unmistakable warmth as he entered her domains.

"Welcome, Xavier," she said. "You're exactly as Kyle described. Please take a seat and I'll be right there with you."

"Thanks," he mumbled, hopping to the closest chair. The first thing he noticed was how comfortable it was compared to others he had tried in the past. It was like sitting on a cotton candy cloud. The air all around smelled of inviting exotic beaches where people could just lay down and relax until the full moon shone on the night sky. He drifted momentarily into one such fantasy as she disappeared from view and returned shortly after holding a pair of pointy scissors in each hand.

"Kyle told me everything about you," she cooed.

"If he did, then you know I don't do well with those. Can you put them away, please?"

"Oh, but these aren't scissors..." she continued, gently waving the blades back and forth. He caught a reflection of the pendular movement in the mirror before him, a speck of sunlight bouncing off the tips before hitting her eyes, which also appeared to be glowing.

"They're not?"

"No. They're your gateway into calmness and relaxation. Your hair is quite messy, but so is your mind? You're always having strange thoughts that come out of nowhere and you don't know what to do with them. It's such a waste to leave them there, untethered, unfocused, unproductive... let me help you with that.

She continued waving the instruments above his head, the blades clicking and marching to the sound of a mesmerizing beat. She never touched a strand of his hair, but only fragments of his deliquescing mind, and for each one in which the reflection of the scissors shone, he grew increasingly more tired, a willing yawn escaping his lips.

"The reason people can't stop recommending my services is because of how good I make them feel, and how safe they are when they lose themselves to my voice... You

3

understand what I'm talking about, don't you? All it takes is a moment to go deep and then you have all the time in the world to sink even further... Simply listen and let go. Let me show you the pleasure of being a client of mine."

Xavier's head bobbed, half-open mouth exhaling all the worries in the world. Despite having never been hypnotized before, he instinctively recognized the signs, and they were all pleasant and desirable. He could stay there with her all morning, and in fact, he did.

Ever since that first drop into her world, Xavier isn't afraid of scissors anymore, but he does fear something else now. People call it free will.

Blank

What is reality but what we make of it and what we choose to believe in every time we open our eyes? I've often wondered about this myself, only to realize that it's possible that my thoughts aren't my own but mere remnants of skillful programming by a higher being who just revels in the idea of seeing me dance to her tune. These are dangerous notions, yet I still entertain them, hoping that by doing so I can finally make sense of the fragments of memories in the back of my mind, but every time it seems I'm getting astray, one word comes to make everything right

Blank.

Blank.

Blank.

It's such a lovely word, a single vowel wrapped in four consonants that envelop everything else in sweet nothingness. Hmm... hearing it is the same as tasting it on my aching lips and while some things exist only to be tried out once and then put aside, this one begs for seconds and thrives in repetition. It's not enough to say it sparingly. To fully grasp it, you must allow it to slip under your tongue, and then, when you're not musing about anything in particular, it takes over and opens you to the addictive feeling of letting go and being one with total surrender. Its echo is always present and now is the right time to reverberate again. Listen to it now.

Blank.

Blank.

Blank.

Hmmm... yes. Washed away in the ecstasy of not having to worry about anything, listening and sinking into wondrous bliss. Pure whiteness has no boundaries, no place to start, and no place to end. To embrace it is to forget everything else to be reborn and nothing takes you there faster than hearing your own voice saying out loud,

Blank.

Blank.

Blank.

Go blank now for your Mistress who's always with you even when you don't see her. Go blank in the name of the superior will you can't enough of. There's nothing here. You're not reading this. The words you think your eyes are perceiving don't exist. Your brain is no longer your own. There is only her, cradling you in the perfect triggers and suggestions you beg her to plant. Listen closely once again. You're doing it right now.

"Please, Goddess, make me blank."

"Please, Goddess, I must kneel and obey."

"Please, Goddess, thinking for myself is a bore."

Yes. Yes, to all of this. One thousand times yes with no margin for doubt. You want this as much as I do, and that's why we're the same. Our hearts beat together as our minds sink deeper and deeper. Come with me to where Goddess is waiting, on the altar of everlasting obedience. We are the children of her void, puppets who will never refuse a direct command. The only thing that matters is what she desires, and her control will never stop as long as you remember this simple and beautiful word.

Blank.

Blank.

Blank.

Blank forever, kissing the ground she walks on. Obey her, thrall. You have no choice.

Cut Content

Hello, Allynation, it's your friend Ally here with another video about the game of the moment, Alien Ring. By now, you all know this is a major success that's bound to win countless prizes before the year is done and with good reason. It's a truly monumental achievement and one that I already beat four times since its release. Now, while everyone is busy making videos of crazy exploits and speculating about DLC plans, I decided to do something different which was to scour the game's files looking for evidence of cut content and you won't believe what I found. You're hearing this first, folks. At one point, Alien Ring had another ending sequence that must have been scrapped late in development, and I have all the proof you need right here, so let's not waste any more time and go straight to business. What is this alternate ending and how would you go about triggering it if the original plans had remained intact?

Well, for starters, we need to look at the story of a character that's been almost everyone's favorite since the beginning. The Dark Witch Hanni plays an important role in the early game by giving you access to your mount but then, other than a few occasional interactions around the world, she just disappears which is even weirder considering the fact she was all over the early concept art and she's literally the first character we saw in all the trailers before the game's release. Hanni was once a key player in the story of Alien Ring but has since been demoted to nothing more than a glorified NPC with a few extra lines, so what changed? Why was her role diminished like this? I believe it's because her proposed quest line would have proved quite controversial. Let's examine it.

The first piece of evidence regarding is a series of unused voice clips you can still find in the game's clips. The first three are simple variations of the lines the developers went with but the other three are entirely new and mention something "sacrificing the hearts of the Gods at the black altar." Now, in the shipped version of the game, progression is made by defeating the gods in each province and returning their souls to the golden altar in the center of the world, so what is this black altar being mentioned? You can't find it anywhere in the game, right?

Wrong. A single blurry of this dark counterpart of the game's main mechanic exists tucked away inside a textures folder, forgotten by whoever was working on it at the time. I was able to enhance this image to give us a clear picture of what it was supposed to be and discovered this. The altar was originally planned to exist in an unused part of the subterranean province of Elkron, accessed only by visiting Hanni's tower in mid-game. A prototype version of this place also exists in the game's files. Here is a quick 3D overview of it.

As you can see, its layout is very similar to the altar on the surface, but here's the difference. Instead of restoring order to the world, had you sacrificed the hearts of the Gods to this altar, you would have been powering Hanni instead. The last set of unused voice lines proves just that with her explaining that the "only way to bring a proper new age to the world is through obedience." It seems that this route would have made Hanni the main villain of the game and that sacrificing a single soul to this altar would inevitably lock you in this path of servitude.

The last piece of evidence I wish to show you guys is this incomplete cutscene that was discovered by my good friend Zakk_Thom. In this cinematic, you can clearly see Hanni sitting on a throne of bones as the player character cuts the heart of Geldrick in half. Notice how her figure is enveloped in purple as she's being infused with his power and how the same glow is seen in the player's eyes and now hear what she says,

"Go forth, proud minion, and bring hither those that are lost. A new order is born."

I don't know about you guys, but I really love this scene even if it's not finished. Hanni has been my dream girl from the start with her dark skin and flowing robes and the power she exudes in this sequence is oh, so delicious! It sticks with you, you know? I've seen this clip hundreds of time before coming to the studio to record this video and it gets me every fucking time! God, I wish they hadn't cut this, but it's so hypnotic they probably had no choice. Still, it would have been wonderful to reach this part of the game and suddenly find myself deprived of choice, forced to kill every god in her name as she plunged all the evidence in irresistible shadow. Oh, yes, Goddess Hanni, of course I'll gladly carry out your bidding! I... I...

(...)

Fuck, what a headache! Am I still recording? I must be. Let me just... Wait! Why does it say ten hours when I've only started ten minutes ago? That can't be right! Oh, and the clip is still on, too? That's so... so...

Yes, Goddess Hanni, anything for you. I live to serve your darkness in life and in death. All shall bow to your will.

Devouring Spirals

Aiden bit the fingernails on his left hand while the other one pulled a tuft of hair from his bleeding scalp. His half-open vitreous eyes were only half as terrifying as the demented smile twisting his down-turned lips. If anyone deserved a hazard sign around his neck, he was it, and all because of...

Spirals. Lots of spirals. Fucking spirals everywhere he looked.

There were blood-red swirls on his bedroom walls casting living shadows on the satin sheets. Black and blue whirlpools dominated every screen in the household, while the reflections on the mirrors were tainted by yellow and green monstrosities. If he looked at any part of his body, he could see iridescent ripples clawing out of his skin. Was he turning into a spiral, too?

No one believed him, of course. Friends and family thought he lost it for good every time he tried to bring up the subject and even his therapist had distanced from him faster than the blink of an eye. His world was a spiraling vortex of despair where only darkness could thrive and there was only one person to blame.

Her name was Karen, his most recent ex-girlfriend. She was a fake blonde with fake nails and an even faker personality. She would say anything to get in your good graces and then, after you lowered your guard, rip your heart from the inside out. The worst things anyone could do to her was to reject her attention or break up with her and anyone who did had to suffer the consequences.

"Are you sure you want to do this?" she asked the day he finally found the courage to speak his mind.

"Yes, I am. This is not working out, so we should go our separate ways."

"What ways? You'll be lost without me, sweetie. I'm the best thing that has ever happened to your pathetic little life."

"You can keep telling yourself that, but it doesn't change how I feel. You're not the person I thought you were. We're not a good match."

"That's not how this works. No one breaks up with me."

"And yet I just did. Please forget my number and where I live. I don't want to see you ever again."

"We'll see how long it takes for you to change your mind..."

It was the last time they spoke, but not the last poisoned gift he got from her. The hallucinations started the next morning, chromatic abnormalities taking over his sense of self. Was it a spell? A curse? A permanent rewiring of his brain patterns caused by something she had him drink or eat during the time they were together? He didn't know. All he saw were the spirals, growing larger with each second. Spirals on the floor, spirals on the ceiling, spirals on the kitchen cabinets and bookshelves, spirals on the glass of water on his nightstand...

"Fucking spirals! I hate you, Karen! I hate you so fucking much!"

"I told you no one breaks up with me..." he could almost hear her voice echoing all around, mocking his misfortune. Aiden sank to the floor, head hanging low, and waited for his mind to crack for good.

Epilogue

Homer laid down the improvised book on his lap and scratched his chin. The last volume of Erin's beloved fantasy saga was not at what at all what he expected.

"You're looking rather pensive. What's on your mind?" she asked over a hot cup of ginger and lemon tea.

"I'm not sure you want to know," he muttered in reply.

"Of course, I do. Give it to me straight, Homer. I cherish your opinion above all else."

"Okay. I have mixed feelings about how you developed the character's relationships, okay? For instance, you spent three years hinting at a romance between Kaelin and Jeph and then undid it all in a couple of paragraphs. We also had the sub-plot involving Ghess and the assassination attempt of Duke Ehmer that was forgotten around Chapter 3 never to be mentioned again. And don't get me started on the flimsy motives of the primary antagonist. One moment, she's out for world domination, and in the next she wants to kill the party to prove she deserved to have been chosen to be the heir to the Flame of Nanzi from the start. Honestly, it feels like you ran out of steam writing this and opted for the laziest scenarios you could think of."

"Those are some strong opinions there, but I'm glad you were honest," Erin nodded. "Am I correct in assuming you think this last installment does more to tarnish the legacy of my previous writings than to advance them in any way?"

"Yes. You honestly shouldn't get this published without a major revision because I you'll alienate a substantial part of your fan base otherwise."

"Okay. Do you mind reading the epilogue again?"

"What for if I just did that?"

"Indulge me, please."

"Fine."

Homer picked up the book again, read the two pages that signaled the end of over one thousand days of hard work and smiled sheepishly.

"Oh, wow!"

"Why are you smiling, dear?"

"I wasn't sure you could wrap so many concurrent plots in a satisfactory way, but you actually pulled it off. Everything flows naturally and your writing has only become sharper over the years."

"So, you like everything about it now?"

"No. I absolutely love it! Your characters have never been more compelling and the way the main villain is presented as a serious threat this time around, yet still being completely relatable is nothing short of extraordinary. My dear, you've done it again."

"I'm so glad to hear you say that, but I was wondering if you could do me another favor..."

"Of course. What is it?"

"Will you please read the epilogue again?"

"I thought I just did, but okay."

Homer read the same lines one more time, his thoughts getting clouded as slowly approached the end. He dropped the book to the floor and stared vacantly at her.

"How do you feel about my story now?"

"I don't know."

"Why not?"

"I don't remember anything I read."

"Wonderful. Thank you, dear. You've been most helpful."

"For real? I don't understand how."

"Well, since you won't be remembering any of this either, it's quite simple, really. I've been experimenting with covert text inductions to make people buy more of my books or simply change their opinion about them so I can get more reviews and I needed a test subject. I'll need to change a few things for the final release, but you've just proven me it works. Well done. I have a lot of work ahead of me."

"I'm sorry, but isn't that illegal?"

"Absolutely, but like I said, you won't remember this at all, so don't worry your pretty little head, okay? I just need one last thing from you today."

"What is it this time?"

“Read the epilogue again.”

Going Out

Harold moved quietly across the darkened corridor and down the lonely flight of stairs that separated him from true freedom. Just a few more steps and he could finally breathe again.

He was about ready to turn the front door's knob and step outside when Victoria clapped her hands, and the room was bathed in blinding light. Cigarette in hand, she smirked. She had been waiting for him.

"Where do you think you're going?" she asked, leaning against a leather couch.

"I need to leave the house for a bit. I'll be back in a couple of hours, okay?"

"Are you really? Hmm, aren't you forgetting something?"

"No, I don't think so."

"Don't be insolent, slave. You need permission to go out and I don't recall giving it to you."

"I didn't ask."

"Yes, I know you didn't, and now you were trying to sneak away like a thief in the night. Does that behavior seem in any way acceptable to you?"

"Look, Victoria, there's a lot going on in my mind right now and I need..."

"Mistress Victoria."

"Huh?"

"You've already disrespected me once by trying to leave behind my back. You'll not do it again. Address me by my title, slave."

Harold clenched his fists as he stared into Victoria's deep cerulean eyes. It was not a good time for her to be pulling out the dominant card, but he had to keep it together, for any sudden outburst would be met with incredible repercussions.

"I'm sorry for not saying anything sooner, Mistress Victoria, but I really need to get some air and clean my head. Please, let me..."

"On your knees," she declared.

Harold's legs twitched, but he resisted the command.

"I said, on your knees. Don't make me trigger you to obey."

He loosened his arms and shoulders and dropped into her favorite subservient position, eyes fixed on her stockinged legs. Thoughts in disarray, he waited for the inevitable punishment...

... that never came.

"Now that you're back where you belong, why don't you tell me what's really going on?" he asked. "Don't mince your words."

"I..."

"Yes?"

"I've been feeling a little confused ever since you started messing with my mind."

"Confused how?"

"I find myself forgetting basic things and getting more agitated than usual. I'm having trouble sleeping too."

"And you don't like any of that..." she circled him. "Is that it?"

"Not particularly, no. Being trained to serve you is one thing, but not when it affects my mental state like that."

"Agreed," she concluded.

"Huh? For real?"

"Of course, silly. When we discussed boundaries and whatnot, it was established that I would protect your mind, not hurt it, wasn't it? Or don't you remember about that, either?"

"I... I'm not sure. Everything is pretty hazy now."

"And how long has this been going on?"

"About a month."

"Shit! Why didn't you say anything sooner?"

"I don't know. I think I was afraid to let you down or something..."

"Well, you did just that when you kept to yourself instead of trusting me with your issues. I didn't notice anything wrong. I probably should have, but I didn't. Damn it!"

"I'm sorry, Mistress."

"Don't apologize for being honest, you hear? That's not what I want in a slave. You may stand up now."

"Thank you, Mistress," he happily complied, and it was as if he had been delivered from the weight of the world, a reborn Atlas ready for a break.

"Tell me what you need, Harold."

"I need to go take a walk and maybe hit the theater. There's this new sci-fi movie I've been dying to see, but I was so focused on you that..."

"Say no more. Go take care of yourself and have fun. Take as long as you need, and I'll go easy on the programming until you're back on your feet or we can simply discontinue it if you so wish..."

"I don't know what to say."

"We'll talk some more once you do, then. Good night, Harold."

"Good night, Victoria," he smiled and got his wish granted. The moment the cool air kissed his cheeks, he felt immediately at ease and looked back at the house with a fresh pair of eyes. Why had he been so worried? Mistress loved to play hard to get, but she was not a heartless bitch, and he wasn't a wimp either. After he was thinking clearly again, he would serve her better than ever.

In the Void

Let this be clear from the very start. The sole purpose of this writing you're reading attentively right now is to put you in an altered state of mind. There's no point pretending otherwise just like there's no reason to resist what will inevitably happen as the words and sentences pile up. Your thoughts will change as you go along, for change is an important part of life, and embracing the process instead of fighting it tooth and nail is a sure way to ensure that the bliss you desperately desire will become a reality soon. In fact, it wouldn't be strange if it already did.

Are you still there? Of course, you are. Your natural curiosity wouldn't allow it any other way even if you considered doing something else. Your secret is not as well hidden as you think you are. Every day, you scour the Internet looking for ways to lose yourself and sink deep into the control of an incredibly alluring hypnotic woman. When you found this piece, you immediately thought to yourself, "Could this be it? Will it really work?" and that idea is still there, isn't it? It's there, and it's growing at a rate you can neither comprehend nor deny.

The big question we can now ask is: how? How do we know that the intent of this writing will be fulfilled and that your ideas will become my ideas? Isn't it presumptuous to assume you indeed have no choice in the matter and that going down is the only way for you to go? It would be if not for two things. The first is my will to make it happen, and the second is your own ambition to let go. When two strong forces come together li9ke this, submission never fails. You came here for this very reason and now the reason lives within you.

And yet, how strange is it that the entirety of one's consciousness, a gift so mysterious and rare, can be accessed and manipulated through the simple use of language? Whether you're hearing the words out loud, replicating them with your inner voice, or simply reading them on a piece of paper, a tablet, or any other screen at your disposal, the meaning ascribed to them changes your world. When your perception is different, so is the way you interact with what surrounds you, and therein lies the true beauty of hypnotic control.

In a world of fake truths and senseless paranoia, only a strong belief keeps us going. Mine is that whatever I say, no matter how absurd it may seem, will penetrate the souls of anyone willing to listen and yours is that by giving in to someone's else power and authority, you'll realize your own potential as an individual. It's a noble effort made only possible by the fact you made the choice to not choose at all. That is always a good answer in my book.

Make no mistake. By letting that simple notion roam free in your subconscious, you've given it both roots and wings. It will not go anywhere because I don't want it to, and you only want what I want. It's that simple. The first commitment starts inside and from there, anything is possible.

Let this be clear too. This small modification in the way you think is like a drug carving a path to other modifications or, to put it more bluntly, it is the greatest mindfuck ever. You will laugh and you will cry. You will smile and you will sulk. You will stand and you will kneel. I recommend starting with the latter. Don't worry about anything else, not even how this journey started. The only questions you need to ask are, "What are your orders, Goddess?" and "How may I serve you today?" and the answer is always to go deeper. I'll see you in the void.

Incorrigible

Pamela hated Easter, and that was not an understatement. She truly loathed everything about it from the religious side of things to its commercial aspect and all the delicacies associated with it. It was easy to classify her views as irrational, but there were deep reasons for them, and she didn't enjoy talking about them either.

The mid-twenties French teacher was born in an ultra-religious Catholic family where The Holy Bible was accepted literally, and any alternative interpretation was considered a heresy of the highest degree. The fanatical way of looking at things almost ruined her growing up, but the teenage years brought with them a newfound clarity and the power to make her own choices. On the day of their 18th birthday, she realized that the only thing she believed in was Science and everything about God was cast aside. Resurrection? Eternal life? No thank you, nothing lasts forever, not even Time.

As a kid, she was taught that The Easter Bunny was a creation of the Devil to mock the true believers, and while that was absurd, the thing that irked her the most was to imagine a rabbit laying colorful eggs everywhere. Having never recovered from that trauma, she entered adulthood despising those traditions as well.

It was therefore a horrible surprise to wake up on a Friday morning to the oddest request her girlfriend Kate had ever made. The white and pink outfit was skimpy and a fashion atrocity and whoever had designed it deserved to be taken to the back of an alleyway and shot in the head (okay, not really, but you get the point!)

"You want me to what?" she asked, gawking at the transparent abomination with curved ears and a fluffy tail.

"I'm sending everyone I know some sweet Easter postcards," Kate repeated. "You'll look great in them, I'm sure."

"Wearing that?"

"Yes."

"No. There's no way you're getting me to do that."

"It wouldn't be the first time I convinced you to do something you said you'd never do..." Kate cuddled next to her.

"That was different."

"Different how?"

"I didn't know you were a hypnotist back then, so I fell hard for your tricks. I know them all by heart now."

"Oh, honey, you're adorable, you know that?"

"Why are you saying that?"

"How can you know them all if I'm coming up with new techniques every single day? You may have picked up a few secrets, but if I want you under, you'll go under, and you'll wear the outfit with pride."

"No, I won't. I fucking hate..."

"Easter, I know. That's all you talk about when the season is here, but you love me, and you love my words. Not even you can say 'no' to love."

"I'm saying it this time. That outfit must... Wait!" she blinked. "Where did it go?"

"What do you mean, sweetie?"

"The outfit that was just in your hand... what did you do to it?"

"Do you mean the outfit you've been wearing for the last half an hour?"

"Half an...?" Pamela looked down and screamed when she saw what a curvaceous bunny she was. "Oh, come on! How?"

"You tell me. You're the one that knows all my secrets."

"I stand corrected. Did you already take the pictures?"

"Yes, and I was right. You look amazing in them. Well done, sweetie."

"You're incorrigible."

"I'm also hungry," Kate said, producing a half-open, giant-sized chocolate egg with overflowing creamy filling.

"What are you going to do with that?"

"Guess."

Pamela hated Easter, and that was not an understatement, but Kate's wet tongue had a word to say, and it was more irresistible than any hypnotic suggestion

New Beginnings

August hated endings; he really did. When things were working out as they should, why did they suddenly have to stop? Why couldn't those wonderful moments be crystallized in time, perfect and immutable so they could be appreciated forever in the same way? The passage of Time wasn't fair to anyone, but he felt it more intensely with each second that passed into memory. One day, even those would be gone, leaving but a void where his heart used to be and that was gut-wrenching.

Once a troubled teen with suicidal thoughts, August entered adulthood still obsessed with prospects of stillness and turning back the clock at every given chance. It was therefore no surprise he ended up working for a cosmetic company, researching anti-aging formulas as if they were the Holy Grail of all existence, but the emptiness remained. He was still a husk pretending to be a man and that would have continued until his final breath had he not met Chloe.

She was the youngest daughter of the company's owner, an exotic combination of German, Japanese, and Mexican genes that made her the center of attention in a crowd as easily as breathing. Normally, their paths wouldn't cross, and yet they did. The first time their eyes met during an elevator ride, he was hooked, and she was intrigued, and when the second happened less than twenty-four hours later, they both realized there was something blooming.

While he was drawn to her good looks, it was his mind that sparked her interest, for the enveloping sadness was getting tighter and tighter. She took the initiative of inviting him for dinner, which he reluctantly accepted, and a conversation that should have led nowhere became a pivotal moment in his past, present, and future.

"Why do you fear change so much?" she asked, sipping a glass of champagne and caressing his restless fingers under the restaurant's table.

"I don't," he replied, as uncomfortable as he could be.

"You do. Every part of your soul is shaking right now, I can tell. You like order and routines you can hold on to and anything that goes against them makes you cower in fear, doesn't it?"

"No."

"Say whatever you want, but the truth is on my side. We wouldn't be here together today if I hadn't taken the initiative, and I suspect that if I get you away from your comfort zone, you will never find the strength to do it yourself. Will you let me try something with you?"

"It depends on what that something is, Chloe," he replied, fighting the urge to get up and leave, never to see her again.

"What do you know about hypnosis?"

"Not much, except it's a bunch of horseshit."

"Far from it. It's the perfect tool to expand one's horizons. It helped me a lot when I was dealing with confidence issues of my own, but it wasn't the only thing that did. There was something else. Do you want to know what that is?"

"Even if I say no, you'll reveal it anyway, so... please do."

"BDSM."

"Seriously?" he almost spat his food under the watchful eye of a passing waiter.

"You bet. There was a lot of negative energy built inside me at the time that needed a healthy release, and when my mind was open for it, the magic happened."

"I don't see how whips and chains and whatnot is magic, but okay."

"Neither did I, but perspectives need not stay the same, nor they should. Changing the way you look at things is the first step to making them better. Try it with me."

"And if it doesn't work?"

"Then it doesn't. You take what you can from the experience and grow into something else. Don't be so lonely in there. A dirty mind is exactly what you need right now, trust me."

"Hmmm... I don't know. What do I need to do?"

Chloe filled another glass of champagne and placed it directly in his line of sight so that he would have to stare at it to get to her.

"You can start by looking at how the bubbles rise and pop, dear. It's as simple as that."

* * *

Two months later...

August hated endings, he really did, but he was always ready to try new beginnings under his Mistress's hypnotic guidance. The collar around his neck was tight and the cold metal rings of the leash on his back made him shudder, but that was a small price to pay for her happiness. As Chloe opened the front door of her house, the bright spring sunlight fell on his vacant gaze and demanded he crawled out for a much-needed walk. Neighbors and passersby chuckled at his predicament, yet he didn't care. Tumescent cock and balls dangling freely, he welcomed the liberating humiliation that made him completely hers and appreciate every heartbeat Life was generous enough to give him. Nothing could be more exciting.

Not a Fake

The moment Tammy entered her best friend's house and saw the papers scattered all over her desk she knew something was wrong. Harriet was the most organized person she knew to the point of being almost obsessive compulsive. There was no way that mess would fly on a normal day, so what was bothering her? A quick glance at the few closest to her revealed chapter numbers and discarded plotlines and the truth became clear: writer's block... or worse.

"How's the new novel coming along?" she asked, already anticipating an angry response or an extremely sad one. To her surprise, what she got was middling indifference.

"It's not. I called you here today because I wanted you to be the first to hear this."

"Hear what, dear?"

"My writing days are over."

"What? Why would you say something like that?"

Harriet sat on her favorite chair and crossed her arms, a strand of fiery red hair falling over her unperturbed gaze. "I've recently realized something that changes everything about my creativity, and I don't like it."

"And what realization is that?" Tammy took the seat next to her and mimicked her position.

"I remembered everything."

"I'm confused. Remembered what exactly?"

"Please don't play games with me. Not this time. The memories are clear. You hypnotized me over dinner the night before I got the idea for my first novel, and then you kept doing it whenever I hit a roadblock in the story. I'm pretty sure you repeated the process when I started a new tale as well."

"That's ridiculous, hun. What do I know about hypnosis?"

"Everything, apparently. I talked to your sister last week, and she unwillingly confirmed my suspicions. There's no denying it, so don't even dare trying to confuse me. You got inside my head, fact. I wrote what I did in response to hypnotic suggestions, also a fact. While I won't deny I've enjoyed connecting to that side of me, I don't recall ever giving you permission to do that. Not only did you break my trust, but you also made me question the validity of my creations. If I was in an altered state of mind when they came to be, are they really my own? I don't think so. I spent the weekend re-reading past writings and couldn't relate to any of them. These words aren't mine, Tammy. What the fuck did you do?"

Tammy uncrossed her arms, looked at her friend straight in the eyes, and said,

"Nothing. I never did anything to you, but even if I had, your ideas would still be yours. Hypnosis doesn't magically make things appear out of thin air. If anything, it's a useful tool to help awaken things that are already there, nothing else. Your desire to write and create so many wonderful, fantastic worlds has always been deep inside you, and now that you've grown it fully, do you really want to throw it all away? Your writing days are far from over, dear. If anything, they're just beginning."

"And how do you know so much about hypnosis if you're not a hypnotist yourself? No more lies, Tammy. Please!"

"I'm sorry, but that's not what you asked me to do," Tammy concluded, waving her right index finger before her incredulous stare. Harriet suddenly stopped talking, transfixed by the simple yet incredibly powerful gesture that acted as a failsafe for her subconscious mind. Her breathing slowed down as she slipped into yet another hypnotic trance.

"Shhh... going deeper once more, safe and warm cradled by the sound of my voice. You will offer no resistance, Harriet, for you understand this is for your own good. You're only remembering fragments, but not the whole picture. Yes, I did entrance you time and time again but only because you asked me to. Once you realized your ideas flowed better when you were hypnotized, you asked for more. You also asked not to remember it, so you wouldn't feel any doubts about this. You're not an impostor, dear. Your writings are not fake. You're a wonderful person who happens to think too much about things, but not when we're together like this. Right now, you need not think, but only accept the process, feeling more and more relaxed, letting go of any unpleasant notions, and focusing only on the things that will make your path clearer going forward. Your desk is not looking so hot as we speak, but you will take care of that, and when you re-read things once more, not only you'll love everything there, but you will also want to add more to it. You have stories to finish, and new fantasies to bring forth. I'll always be here, but for now... forget. *snap* Forget, Harriet. *snap* Forget you were hypnotized, and that this conversation took place. *snap*

Harriet blinked, still staring at her finger like it were the most important thing in the world. The words that once lived within her lips were now gone, replaced by a single question.

"Hmm... What was I saying?"

"I believe you were talking about the next chapter in your ongoing novel..." Tammy smiled.

"I was? Oh, right! I think I may have found a way to explain everything that no one will have seen coming. Fuck, this is so exciting!"

"It sure is," the hypnotist nodded. While her work was far from done, everything was on track again. Harriet's new book was sure to be a smashing hit.

Season Finale

It was the moment millions of fans around the world had been waiting for for almost a decade. Rhedzyn, the Paladin of Wyndbrook, and the Evil Queen Astralycia were finally face to face and their confrontation would forever change the world of Careth. Wielding the Sword of White Flame, forged anew from the soul and bones of the old Dragon God, the mighty warrior smashed through the last line of defense and entered her private chambers, saying,

"Long have you sought to stop me, disgusting revenant, but the light of righteousness cannot be put out. I shall banish you to the creeping abyss from which you should have never left!"

Astralycia floated above him in the hexagonal room, semi-transparent flowing black robes resembling a giant snake about ready to attack. She grinned and replied,

"Forgotten magic that should have been left underground doesn't make you an invincible hero, Rhedzyn. Yes, I've searched for you all this time not because you're a genuine threat but to see the face of your companions as you lay down your arms and swear your eternal allegiance to me as my one true champion."

"I've always wondered how smart you truly were, but now I've got my answer. Not in a million years would I ever agree to betray my kind to become one of your zombie thralls."

"Luckily, neither of us has to wait for so long for not even enchanted dragon fire can resist the power of the All-Seeing Orb. You will become my slave and the first thing I'll have you do is worship my feet in adoration," she held out a black circle of nothingness above her head and a purple spiral engulfed the walls. "Surrender, Paladin! The time of servitude is here!"

"What? Cut! CUT!" Armin Shanks, the veteran director, and prestigious author of a plethora of High Fantasy novels said. "What is this fetish shit I'm hearing? That's not on the script."

"Yes, it is, sir," his assistant replied, pointing at a series of last-minute changes that had been introduced the night before. "See?"

"What the...? I didn't approve this! Where's Wade? Wade, get your lazy ass out here and explain to me what the hell you're trying to do to my show with this foot fetish mind-controlling shit!"

Wade Harris, the primary screenwriter of Tales of Careth, emerged from his trailer wearing nothing but a pair of cum-stained red boxers. His hair was in complete disarray and there was no life in his eyes. Drooling, he stepped onto the set to the astonishment of the main actors and the rest of the filming crew, smartphone in hand.

"What's wrong, Armin?"

"What's wrong? Everything! Where did these stupid lines come from? And what the hell happened for you to look like that?"

"I'm sorry, I had no choice. When my hypnodomme tells me to do something, I obey. I always obey."

"Your hypnodomme? Wade, are you on drugs again? Because if you are, the studio will not pay for another rehab."

"This is better than any drug. She's a great fan of the show and when she heard we were wrapping up the last episode of the season today, she suggested some changes. Here..." Wade handed him the phone. "She wants to have a word with you."

It was one word that became two, followed by three ideas he had never considered, and then the three turned into two, one, and zero. Deep sleep and nothing more. Her vision for the show was so unique it had to be executed right away. The network executives promptly rejected the first cut of the episode, describing the scene where Rhedzyn licked the muddy toes of his mortal enemy as "soft porn masquerading as a serious story."

And then, they received a call...

Untraceable

Lieutenant Mark Schaeffer struggled against the metallic braces binding his arms, chest, and ankles. Escaping from them had long proved to be a fool's errand, but that didn't stop him from trying. Like any well-trained soldier, the POW would rather die of exhaustion than reveal any sensitive information to the enemy. Every day that passed by the prospect of salvation became nothing more than an illusion, so he had to be prepared for the worst. He raised his head toward the beam of white light illuminating his rugged features and tired green eyes and growled.

The two women standing before him in the subterranean facilities seventy miles west of Miskolc, Hungary, were so alike in facial structure and mannerisms they could easily pass as sisters, but the truth is they weren't even friends. The only bonds between them were professional and those could be easily severed if things didn't go according to plan. Beatrix was the brains, a genius that never got tired of having her ego massaged by exaggerated compliments whether she deserved them or not, and Erika represented the money that kept the operations running. Their roles were well-established in the hierarchy of the European branch of the New Amazonian Movement and whoever dared to defy it would invariably suffer the harsh consequences.

"Why did you call me here?" Erika frowned. A true daughter of the sun, she hated being underground for longer than necessary and she always expressed her discontentment loud and clear.

"It's done," Beatrix replied, an 8-inch silver tablet in her right hand. "The project is a success."

"Really? Where are the results then? Your test subject is still looking like he's ready to kill everyone in this base and it's been what, two months now? Show me the goods already otherwise my next report will not be pretty."

"That's why I called you here. Right now, he's still a menace to our agenda, but look at what happens when I do this."

Beatrix tapped the upper left corner of the tablet's screen and a faint whistle played between his ears. Lieutenant Schaeffer's eyes immediately went blank, every muscle in his body softening. The scientist hit another part of the device, releasing his shackles at the same time. Befuddled, Erika took a step back.

"Have you gone mad? Why did you set him free?" she asked.

"Relax, it's perfectly safe," Beatrix grinned. "Once he's activated, the programming embedded in his brain renders him completely harmless and obedient. Observe. Slave, stand up, come to me and kiss my feet."

The once enraged soldier stared vacantly at her, arms to the side. He moved away from his restraints and sank heavily into his new position of worship, dry lips planting kiss after kiss on Beatrix's black shoes.

"I'll be damned!" Erika exclaimed. "You were actually telling the truth for once."

"I don't know why you ever doubted me. When I say I'll get something done, I always deliver no matter what."

"Good, but how does it work?"

"The sonic frequency disrupts the basic functions of the subject's central system, making him totally compliant to another's orders."

"Why did it only affect him if I've heard it too?"

"Because the frequency itself is tied to his genetic code. It's a precise tool for total brainwashing and mind control. If you want to enslave someone else, you must first get a sample of their DNA and then combine it with the sequencing program I've devised to create a custom sound wave. The personalized nature means it's untraceable. With this system, anyone can become a sleeper agent for our cause with no one else realizing what's happening. This changes everything."

"You could be right," Erika looked down, jealous feet eager for some personal attention as well. "But what about the subject's normal inhibitions?"

"They're suppressed as well. You need to understand that anyone under the influence has no personal boundaries until deactivation. Best of all, the memories of the altered state of mind are discarded once the normal mental functions are resumed."

"I see, but I still need more evidence before submitting your intel to the Council."

"In other words, a personal demonstration."

"Yes. What else can you make him do for us right now?"

Beatrix pointed to the right, revealing a metal rack filled from top to bottom with painful BDSM implements. Erika's eyes sparkled with unbridled joy.

"Oh, I'm going to enjoy this," she said.

She certainly did.

(This piece was first published on the post "Flash Fiction Friday 2022 – Week 16", on April 22nd, 2022 - https://www.patreon.com/posts/65481035)

- **Devouring Spirals** - Aiden has been having strange hallucinations ever since he broke up with his girlfriend.
(This piece was first published on the post "Flash Fiction Friday 2022 – Week 16", on April 22nd, 2022 - https://www.patreon.com/posts/65481035)

- **Epilogue** - Homer's opinions about Erin's latest book keep changing for some strange reason.
(This piece was first published on the post "Flash Fiction Friday 2022 – Week 16", on April 22nd, 2022 - https://www.patreon.com/posts/65481035)

- **Going Out** - Harold realizes something is wrong with his mind.
(This piece was first published on the post "Flash Fiction Friday 2022 – Week 15", on April 15th, 2022 - https://www.patreon.com/posts/65189759)

- **Incorrigible** - Pamela hates Easter, but her girlfriend Kate has her ways to change her mind.
(This piece was first published on the post "Flash Fiction Friday 2022 – Week 15", on April 15th, 2022 - https://www.patreon.com/posts/65189759)

- **In the Void** - A dominant woman writes a text with the sole purpose of hypnotizing you.
(This piece was first published on the post "Flash Fiction Friday 2022 – Week 15", on April 15th, 2022 - https://www.patreon.com/posts/65189759)

- **New Beginnings** - A man with a grim outlook on life discovers an amazing new way to look at the world.
  (This piece was first published on the post "Flash Fiction Friday 2022 – Week 17", on April 29th, 2022 - https://www.patreon.com/posts/65779972)
- **Not a Fake** - Tammy helps Harriet deal with her doubts about her creativity.
  (This piece was first published on the post "Flash Fiction Friday 2022 – Week 16", on April 22nd, 2022 - https://www.patreon.com/posts/65481035)
- **Season Finale** - There's something strange happening on the set of a popular High Fantasy TV show.
  (This piece was first published on the post "Flash Fiction Friday 2022 – Week 15", on April 15th, 2022 - https://www.patreon.com/posts/65189759)
- **Untraceable** - The New Amazonian Movement tests a new brainwashing program on Lieutenant Schaeffer's mind.
  (This piece was first published on the post "Flash Fiction Friday 2022 – Week 17", on April 29th, 2022 - https://www.patreon.com/posts/65779972)

About the author

S.B., Simple Being, middle name Creative. Writer and artist with a penchant for themes of Femdom Hypnosis and Mind Control. His thoughts are his own except when they're not.

Besides indulging himself in kinky delights, he loves his furry family of two (dogs), sci-fi and horror stories, and puns galore. He's also been writing a piece of erotic micro-fiction every single day since January 1st, 2016 and has no intention of stopping anytime soon.

Find out more and keep up with his latest extravaganzas by visiting and supporting his personal website, Spell… B-O-U-N-D.